# GRAPHIC NATURAL DISASTERS
# TSUNAMIS & FLOODS

by Gary Jeffrey

The Rosen Publishing Group, Inc., New York

Published in 2007 by The Rosen Publishing Group, Inc.
29 East 21st Street, New York, NY 10010

**First edition, 2007**

Designed and produced by
David West Books

*Editor:* Gail Bushnell

Photo credits:
p6b, David Rydevik; p7m, U.S. Navy photo by Photographer's Mate 2nd Class Philip A. McDaniel; p7r, NASA; p44m, U.S. Navy photo by Photographer's Mate 3rd Class James R. McGury ; p44b, Photo by Andrea Booher/FEMA Photo;  p45t, Photograph courtesy of the Pacific Tsunami Museum in Hilo; p45m, NOAA.

### Library of Congress Cataloging-in-Publication Data

Jeffrey, Gary.
  Tsunamis and floods / by Gary Jeffrey ; illustrated by Gary Jeffrey.
    p. cm. -- (Graphic natural disasters)
  ISBN-13: 978-1-4042-1990-8 (library binding)
  ISBN-10: 1-4042-1990-0 (library binding)
  ISBN-13: 978-1-4042-1980-9 (6 pack)
  ISBN-10: 1-4042-1980-3 (6 pack)
  ISBN-13: 978-1-4042-1979-3 (pbk.)
  ISBN-10: 1-4042-1979-X (pbk.)
  1. Tsunamis. 2. Floods. I. Title.
  GC221.2.J44 2007
  904'.5--dc22

                            2006030857

Manufactured in China

# CONTENTS

# WHAT IS A TSUNAMI?

If a large volume of the ocean is quickly displaced, it will sometimes create a huge wave known as a tsunami.

## CREATING A MONSTER

The Earth's crust is cracked all over, forming a number of plates. These plates are continually moving against each other, very slowly. Friction can cause plates to "stick." Eventually, the force building up overcomes the friction and the plates shudder, creating an earthquake. If this happens under the ocean it can create a tsunami. Volcanic islands, erupting violently, can dump thousands of tons of rock into the ocean creating a tsunami. In the distant past large meteors landed in the ocean, creating massive tsunamis.

*Japan is on a major fault line. Tsunami is a Japanese word meaning "harbor wave." Japanese fishermen returning from the open sea, would be amazed to find their harbor utterly destroyed after a tsunami.*

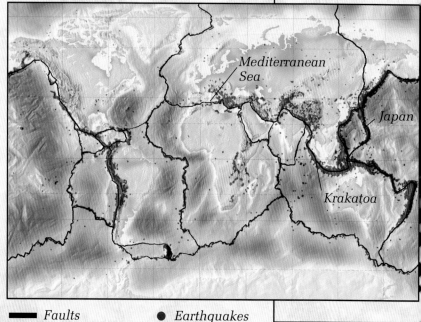

*The world map shows the Earth's plates separated by cracks known as faults. Most earthquakes, shown as red dots, happen along these fault lines.*

Mediterranean Sea

Japan

Krakatoa

— Faults    ● Earthquakes

4

Although rare, volcanic islands have been responsible for some major tsunamis. In 1883, the volcanic island of Krakatoa exploded and then collapsed into the ocean. Several cubic miles of ocean were displaced, creating a series of massive tsunamis. A Greek island in the Mediterranean Sea, today called Santorini, exploded in 1650 B.C., creating a tsunami that devastated the Minoan culture on the nearby island of Crete.

The famous Japanese artist, Hokusai, portrayed a tsunami in the 19th century (above).

Volcano collapses into the ocean

Tsunami

The force of plate movement overcomes friction and the crust jolts upward

Tsunami

The 2004 Asian tsunami was created by the crust rising along 750 miles (1,207 km) of fault line under the ocean. Seven cubic miles (11 cubic km) of ocean was displaced, raising the world's sea level by 0.004 inches (0.1 mm).

# WHY ARE TSUNAMIS DANGEROUS?

In the open ocean a tsunami may go unnoticed. Its wave height is generally less than three feet (one meter) high, but when it reaches shallow water it can reach heights of 120 ft (37 m).

### WAVE TRAIN

Tsunamis are quite often a series of waves called a "train." Unlike wind-blown waves, a tsunami travels at speeds of about 500 mph (805 km/h) but slows down to about 45 mph (72 km/h) when it reaches shallow water. This is still too fast to outrun! The destructive power comes from the mass of water traveling behind the wave. As the wave hits the coast it continues onward, crushing buildings in its path.

*A village near the coast of Sumatra, Indonesia, lies in ruins in the wake of the Asian tsunami, 2004.*

*People flee as the tsunami hits the coast at Ao Nang in Thailand on December 26, 2004.*

**2.** *As the tsunami reaches shallower water it begins to slow down. The wave wall gets steeper as it gets higher.*

**3.** *As it approaches the coast the water is sucked away from the beaches (B). The water height rises as the wave wall becomes steeper.*

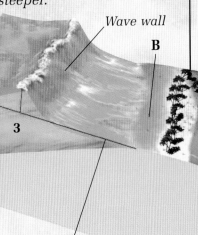

Wave wall

B

3

Normal
sea level

# FLOODS

**R**ivers will burst their banks and flood the countryside as part of nature's course. The Ancient Egyptians relied on the Nile flooding once a year to enrich the soil of the farmland. Today the monsoon floods large parts of Bangladesh once a year.

## MODERN TIMES

Large-scale flooding disasters have become more numerous in modern times as more people live close to rivers. Many towns and cities are next to the rich farmland on flood plains and sometimes dikes have had to be built to protect these areas. This will often increase a river's flooding potential further downstream. Rivers normally flood as a result of natural factors like heavy rainfall or melting snow.

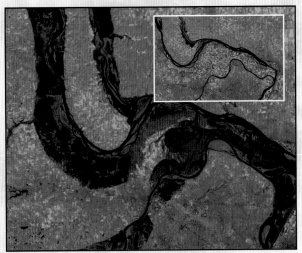

*A satellite view of the Great Midwestern Flood of 1993 (above), and the Mississippi and Missouri rivers before the flood (inset).*

# THE GREAT MIDWESTERN FLOOD OF 1993

FOR MUCH OF ITS 2,300 MILE (3,701 KILOMETER) LENGTH THE MISSISSIPPI RIVER IS KEPT IN ITS CHANNEL BY MAN-MADE BARRIERS.

THESE BARRIERS, CALLED LEVEES, ALLOW PEOPLE TO USE LAND THAT WOULD NORMALLY BE FLOODED OFTEN.

THE LEVEE SYSTEM WORKED WELL FROM THE 1930'S TO THE EARLY 1990'S. IN THE SUMMER OF 1993, THE NORMAL WEATHER PATTERN WENT **HAYWIRE**...

WHISPERING OAK FARM, BLACK RIVER FALLS, WISCONSIN, JUNE 16.

THE WEATHER HAS GONE CRAZY! SIX DAYS OF RAIN, AND NO END IN SIGHT!

MARTHA, THAT'S OVER FOUR INCHES OF WATER!

AND AFTER THAT RAINY SPRING WE HAD...

...THE SOIL IS LIKE A WET SPONGE—TOTALLY SATURATED!

THE RUN-OFF IS JUST FILLING UP THE RIVER, WHICH IS ALREADY AT TWO FEET OVER ITS FLOOD STAGE.

JUNE 20...

TORRENTIAL RAINS IN THE MIDWEST HAVE CAUSED CHAOS IN BLACK RIVER FALLS, WISCONSIN, WHEN A LEVEE BURST, DROWNING OVER 100 PROPERTIES...

IF THIS RAIN DOESN'T STOP, WE'RE GOING TO BE IN FOR ONE HECK OF A BATH!

**Dawn Fratangelo**     **NBC**

STOP

JULY 22...

PANIC IN ST. LOUIS, A CITY WHICH HAS BEEN ON FLOOD ALERT FOR 25 DAYS! EARLY THIS MORNING A LEAK APPEARED IN THE FLOODWALL HOLDING BACK THE MISSISSIPPI.

ARMY CORPS ENGINEERS ARE WORKING FURIOUSLY TO PATCH UP THE FAILING PANEL. THE FLOODWALL HAS BEEN DESIGNED TO HOLD BACK A POSSIBLE CREST OF 52 FEET.

JULY 23, PIKE COUNTY. THE SNY IS THE ONLY UNBROKEN LEVEE LEFT IN THE QUINCY AREA.

I DON'T KNOW HOW MUCH LONGER WE CAN HOLD IT BACK.

THE RIVER'S FORECAST TO RISE ANOTHER TWO FEET IN THE NEXT 48 HOURS!

WHEN THE FLOOD ARRIVES...

IT'S HOLDING—YEAH!!

AUGUST 4...

...AND MORE GOOD NEWS. STE. GENEVIEVE, –"THE TOWN THAT REFUSED TO DROWN," IS FINALLY SEEING THE FLOOD WATERS RECEDE AFTER ITS TEMPORARY LEVEE STAYED INTACT.

THE FLOOD SEEMS TO BE OVER BUT THE COST HAS BEEN ENORMOUS. 48 LIVES LOST, 10,000 HOMES DESTROYED— $15 BILLION WORTH OF DAMAGE.

IN MORE THAN 70 TOWNS ACROSS NINE STATES THE CLEAN-UP BEGINS—EXCEPT IN VALMEYER...

...WHERE THE ENTIRE TOWN IS GOING TO BE REBUILT FROM SCRATCH ON A BLUFF–380 FEET ABOVE THE MISSISSIPPI*.

*IN 1997 NEW VALMEYER WAS OPENED TO RESIDENTS.

THE END

# THE ASIAN TSUNAMI, 2004

CRACK!

RUMBLE!

WHAT'S HAPPENING?

I DON'T KNOW!

AIEE! THE CEILING!

EARTHQUAKE! EVERYBODY GET AWAY FROM THE BUILDINGS!

155 MILES (249 KILOMETERS) SOUTHWEST OF BANDA ACEH, 18 MILES (29 KILOMETERS) BELOW SEA LEVEL, A FAULT LINE IS RUPTURING.

750 MILES (1,207 KILOMETERS) OF SEABED IS BEING FORCED UPWARD BY 65 FEET (20 METERS), CAUSING BILLIONS OF TONS OF WATER TO RISE...

...IN AN INSTANT.

TSUNAMIS HAVE ALSO HIT SIMEULUE, AND ALTHOUGH MOST OF THE 750 INHABITANTS ARE SAFE ON HIGH GROUND, SEVEN ARE KILLED.

PACIFIC TSUNAMI WARNING CENTER (PTWC), HAWAII (70 MINUTES AFTER EARTHQUAKE)...

WE NEED TO REVISE THE BULLETIN WE POSTED AT 3:14. THE INDIAN OCEAN QUAKE IS A LOT STRONGER THAN WE THOUGHT.

PTWC HAD RECEIVED WARNINGS FROM AN EARTHQUAKE TRIGGER ALARM IN AUSTRALIA.

SHOULD I ADD A TSUNAMI WARNING?

...THOUGH WITHOUT SENSORS IN PLACE WE HAVE NO WAY OF KNOWING EXACTLY HOW BIG...

YES, A QUAKE OF THIS MAGNITUDE IS VERY LIKELY TO HAVE TRIGGERED A WAVE...

...NOR DO WE KNOW WHO TO CONTACT IN THE COUNTRIES THAT MIGHT BE AFFECTED.

PATONG BEACH, PHUKET, THAILAND, (89 MINUTES AFTER EARTHQUAKE)...

DID YOU SEE THAT? THE WATER JUST DRAINED RIGHT OUT OF THE BAY!

HNUUH!

HALF AN HOUR LATER THE SURVIVORS ARE AWAITING RESCUE WHEN...

OH NO! LOOK! —LOOK!

ANOTHER WAVE IS COMING!

OH NO, NOT AGAIN!

PTWC HAWAII. FOLLOWING A WIRE SERVICE BULLETIN ABOUT THE TSUNAMI IMPACT IN SRI LANKA, AT 256 MINUTES AFTER THE EARTHQUAKE, PTWC IS FINALLY IN THE LOOP.

IT'S THE SRI LANKAN NAVY. THEY WANT TO BE ALERTED IN CASE OF AFTERSHOCKS.

CHARLES, I THINK YOU'D BETTER COME SEE THIS.

SHENTH RAVINDRA SURVIVES THE SECOND WAVE, BUT OVER 1,700 OTHERS DO NOT. THE QUEEN OF THE SEA HAS BECOME THE WORLD'S WORST TRAIN WRECK.

30,000 IN SRI LANKA, 5,000 KILLED IN THAILAND...

...OVER 80 ON THE MALDIVES ISLAND. THE WAVES EVEN REACHED WEST AFRICA, WHERE AN ESTIMATED 280 PEOPLE HAVE BEEN KILLED, 3,000 MILES FROM THE EARTHQUAKE ZONE.

...12,000 IN INDIA...

42

# WARNINGS & AID

**A**lthough undersea earthquakes can be detected, they do not always create a tsunami. Even when a tsunami is detected, warning remote coastal villages may take too long.

## DEEP OCEAN TSUNAMI DETECTION

After the 1946 Aleutian Island earthquake and resulting tsunami, which hit Hawaii and Alaska, the Pacific Tsunami Warning Center (PTWC) was established in 1949. It has a number of deep water bottom pressure sensors and buoys. There are never any false alarms. When a warning is issued a tsunami is on its way! After the 2004 tsunami, the Indian Ocean warning system was established. But in July 2006, hundreds of people were killed by a tsunami in Indonesia because the alarm did not reach the coast in time.

*Locals run for their lives as a tsunami (in the background) hits Hilo, Hawaii, on April 1, 1946. 165 people in Hawaii and Alaska were killed.*

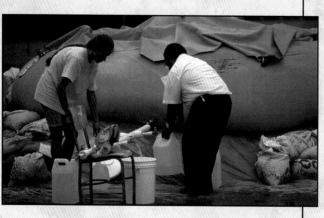

*Getting aid to people quick can reduce death tolls considerably. Locals of Lho Kruet, Sumatra, carry food parcels in the wake of the Asian tsunami (above). Fresh water is delivered to residents in Des Moines, Iowa, (left), after the Great Midwestern Flood contaminated their supplie*

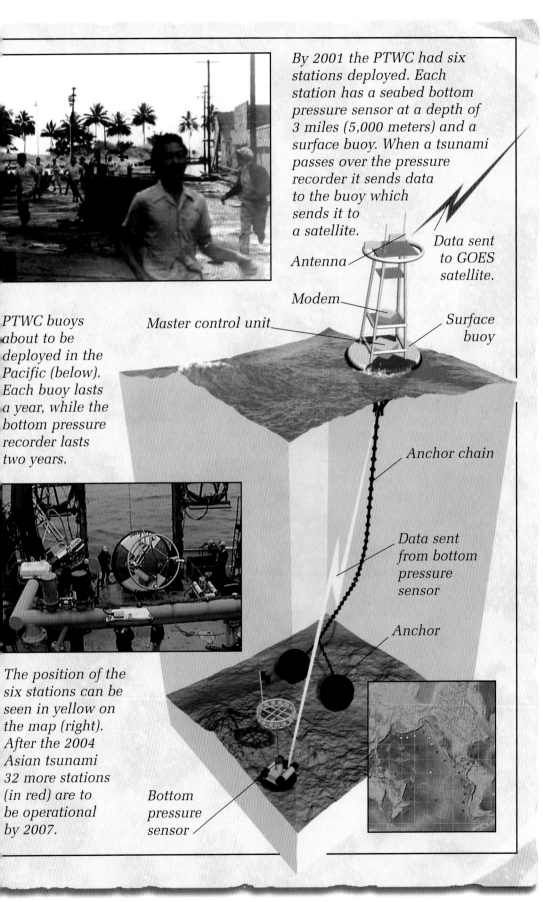

By 2001 the PTWC had six stations deployed. Each station has a seabed bottom pressure sensor at a depth of 3 miles (5,000 meters) and a surface buoy. When a tsunami passes over the pressure recorder it sends data to the buoy which sends it to a satellite.

Antenna

Data sent to GOES satellite.

Modem

Master control unit

Surface buoy

PTWC buoys about to be deployed in the Pacific (below). Each buoy lasts a year, while the bottom pressure recorder lasts two years.

Anchor chain

Data sent from bottom pressure sensor

Anchor

The position of the six stations can be seen in yellow on the map (right). After the 2004 Asian tsunami 32 more stations (in red) are to be operational by 2007.

Bottom pressure sensor

# GLOSSARY

**bulletin** A short, regular news report.

**catastrophe** Disaster.

**contaminated** Made impure by pollution or poisonous substances.

**crest** In this book crest is used to describe the height above sea level the flooding waters will reach.

**data** Information.

**deploy** To put into action.

**devastate** To destroy or ruin.

**Earth's crust** The thin outer layer of the Earth which is up to 40 miles (64 kilometers) thick, but only three miles (5 kilometers) thick under the oceans.

**enormity** The huge scale of something.

**flood plain** An area of flat land that has been created by the sediment from a flooding river.

**friction** The resistance created by one object rubbing against another.

**GOES satellite** A satellite that stays in orbit over the same spot on the Earth.

**humanitarian** Concern for people's well-being.

**levee** An embankment or wall built along a river bank to prevent flooding.

**mandatory evacuation** The enforced moving of people from one area to another because of a danger.

**meteor** Rocks from outer space that fall to Earth. Some are small specks that burn up in the Earth's atmosphere, known as shooting stars. Others can be the size of a mountain, but are very rare.

**meteorologist** A scientist who studies and predicts the atmosphere and its weather.

**Minoan** A civilization that was centered on the island of Crete in the Mediterranean, between 3,000 and 5,000 years ago.

**mooring** A place on a river or lake where boats are tied up.

**potential** Having the possibility to do something in the future.

**recede** To go or move back from a place.

**remote** Far away with limited or no communication.

**temporary** Makeshift. Not lasting a long time.

**volunteer** Someone who offers to work, often for no fee.

# FOR MORE INFORMATION

## ORGANIZATIONS

Pacific Tsunami Museum Inc.
130 Kamehameha Avenue
Hilo, Hawaii 96721
(808) 935-0926
fax (808) 935-0842
tsunami@tsunami.org.
http://www.tsunami.org/index.htm

## FOR FURTHER READING

Carruthers, Margaret W. *Tsunamis* (Watts Library). London, England: Franklin Watts (2005).

Hamilton, John. *Tsunamis* (Nature's Fury). Edina, MN: Abdo & Daughters Publishing (2005).

Langley, Andrew. *Hurricanes, Tsunamis, and Other Natural Disasters* (Kingfisher Knowledge). London, England: Kingfisher, 2006.

Orme, David and Helen Orme. *Tsunamis (What on Earth?: Wild Weather)*. New York, NY: Children's Press, 2005.

Thompson, Luke. *Floods* (High Interest Books). New York, NY: Children's Press, 2000.

Torres, John Albert. *Disaster in the Indian Ocean: Tsunami 2004* (Monumental Milestones: Great Events of Modern Times). Hockessin, DE: Mitchell Lane Publishers, 2005.

Valaire, Nicole. *Our Changing Planet: How Volcanoes, Earthquakes, Tsunamis, and Weather Shape Our Planet* (Scholastic Voyages of Discovery. Natural History, 17). New York, NY: Scholastic Trade, 1996.

Walker, Nikki. *Tsunami Alert!* (Disaster Alert!) Ontario, Canada: Crabtree Children's Books, 2005.

# INDEX

## Web Sites

Due to the changing nature of Internet links, the Rosen Publishing Group, Inc., has
developed an online list of Web sites related to the subject of this book. This site is updated
regularly. Please use this link to access the list:
http://www.rosenlinks.com/gnd/tsfl